CRUEL LOVE

COSA NOSTRA NOVELLA

R.G. ANGEL

Copyright © 2023 by R.G. Angel

All rights reserved.

No portion of this book may be reproduced in any form without written permission from the publisher or author, except as permitted by U.S. copyright law.

Contents

Foreword	IV
Dedication	V
Chapter 1	1
Chapter 2	11
Chapter 3	23
Chapter 4	37
Chapter 5	45
Chapter 6	55
Chapter 7	63
Epilogue	73
About R.G. Angel	77
Also By	78

Foreword

This novella is set in the ***Cosa Nostra*** world. You will be introduced to Gianluca Montanari who is the head of the New York Italian Mafia and the hero of Broken Prince.

With the Cosa Nostra series, be ready to dive into the New-York Italian Mafia through the eyes of Luca, Dom and Matteo and their headstrong heroines in a series filled with ***passion, obsession, revenge, secrets, and drama.***

International Bestselling Author R.G. Angel brings you over 1,000 pages of heart-stopping angst, hot alpha mafia men, strong heroines, steamy moments, and heartbreaks with Happily-ever-after's that will bring you to your knees.

This series includes the following titles:

- **Broken Prince**

- **Twisted Knight**

- **Cruel King**

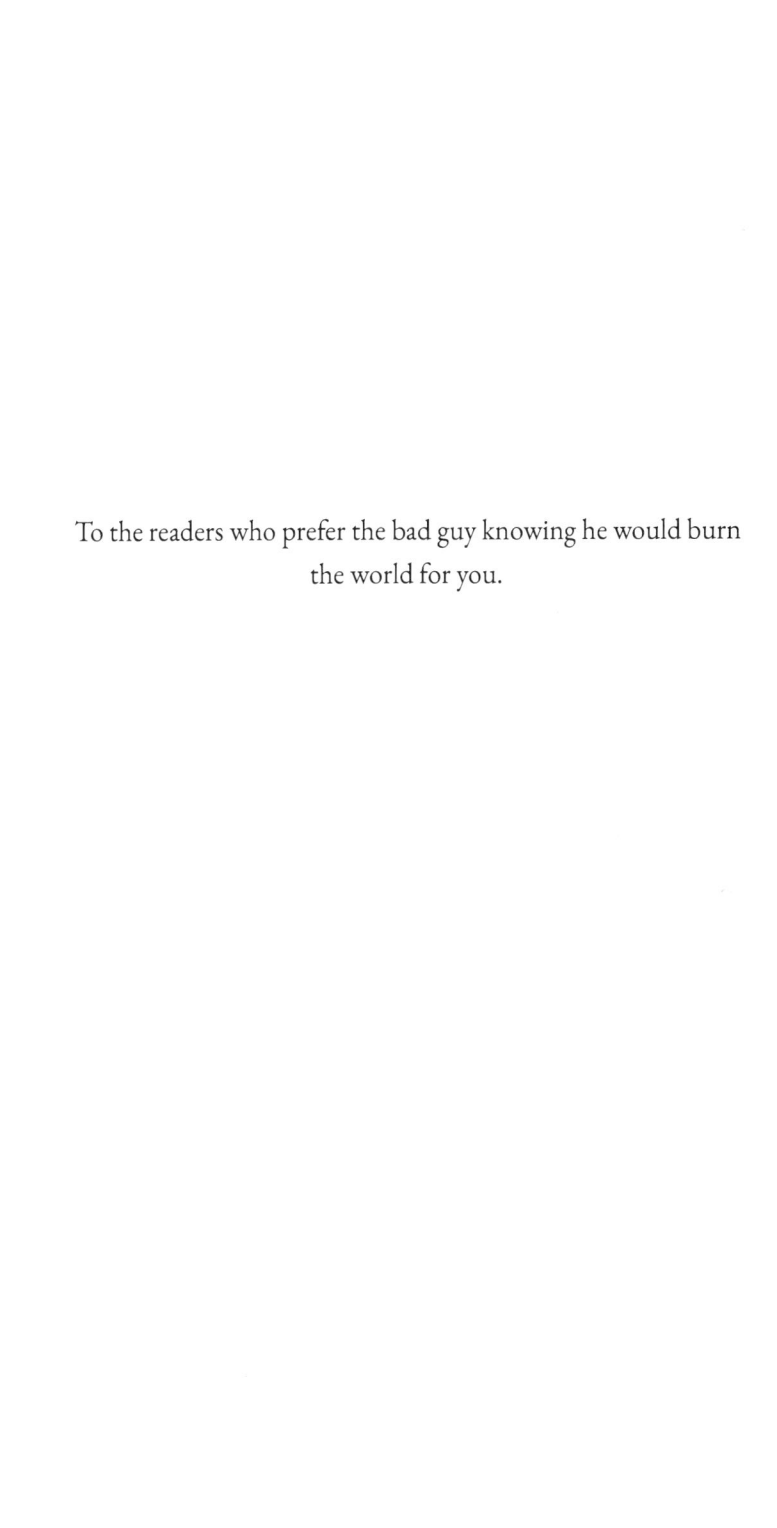

To the readers who prefer the bad guy knowing he would burn the world for you.

Chapter 1

Caly

I froze, and my heart stalled in my chest as I read the angry red paper stuck on the glass door of my small bakery.

'*Eviction Notice—Thirty days before mandatory vacation of the premises.*'

"Caly, what does this mean?" I turned toward Mrs. Mitchell, the elderly owner of the knitting shop beside mine, and saw the identical notice on her door.

I turned around and saw the same notice on all the stores that were still closed across the street.

"Caly?" she asked again, her voice carrying a stress she didn't need especially with her heart condition.

"I'm - I'm not sure Mrs. Mitchell. I was told," My words died in my throat and my eyes finally registered the company name, logo, and electronic signature at the bottom of the page. The crowned viper swallowing a person, I knew by heart, the Visconti coat of arms and the company of the same name, *Visconti International,* along with a signature at the bottom that somehow still hurt me after all these years - *Sebastiano Visconti - CEO.*

"Fucking shit-eating rats! I thought we settled that fucking mess. You said we were okay!"

I took a deep breath and turned around slowly to meet the thundering eyes of Mr. Lucetti-the local butcher and the self-appointed "boss" of *Indie Row.* Yet all the negotiation and speaking tasks always fell on me as I took over from my great-aunt, who'd been the spokeswoman for this neighborhood for over thirty-five years.

"I know just as much as you do," I said calmly, removing the paper from the door. "You were at the consultation as well when King Holding stepped down from the buy-out project."

He looked down at the red paper in his hand and waved it in the air. "Who the fuck is Sebastiano Visconti, anyway?" He balled the page in his fist. "I'm sure it's an old, frustrated, short-dick man"

Mrs. Mitchell gasped at his words, and he waved his hand at her.

"Oh, come on, old bat, you've heard worse! And it's our livelihood that's in danger here! Where will we go?"

"Hey! You don't talk to her like that." I pointed a finger at him.

"Maybe I should go to his office and fuck him up."

I wanted to roll my eyes. Mr. Lucetti still thought he was in his prime when he was an amateur boxer who'd had a little fame in Queens. The yellowing newspaper cutouts framed on his wall could attest to it. He seemed to forget that he was now a middle-aged, overweight, angry man.

He also obviously had no idea who the man he wanted to "fuck up" was. Sebastiano was the opposite of what he'd said. He was the heir of the Las Vegas Mafia, not something I'd been aware of before getting involved with him, and he broke my heart. I could remember him as a twenty-two-year-old, six-foot-four muscular man with a dick that was anything but small, but that had been six years ago. Part of me was certain he looked even more terrifying today than he had been back then.

"You won't need to go fuck up anyone." I looked at my watch. "Becky will be here in a couple of hours. Let me open and get the cakes out, and put some pastries in the oven, and I'll go to the offices there." I tapped the address on the flier with my finger hoping that Sebastiano would still be doing his evil deeds all the way to Vegas, and I could speak to him or go beg Gianluca Montanari, the head of the New York Mafia and my unlikely ally in this whole ordeal.

"Oh, yeah because you fixed it so well last time." He crossed his arms over his chest.

"We're a committee, *Bernie*. I didn't see you stepping up then." I turned to Mrs. Mitchell, smoothing my features. "Don't worry about Twist & Purl, please. I'll find a solution, okay?"

She smiled and patted my cheek with her soft weathered hands. "You're a good egg, sweet girl. Your aunt Milly was lucky to have you."

I smiled at the thought of my great-aunt. A woman who never met me but offered me shelter, love, and support when I needed it the most. The woman who offered me a future when the one I had planned had been annihilated. A woman who allowed me to crawl in her love and heal my wounds—all this because of my first love, the cruelest love of all, Sebastiano Visconti.

The next couple of hours went by in a blur, between the setup for the day, the customers, and the other shop owners who came panicking, expecting me to have a solution to this problem as I did for the last few we had.

Indie Row has not been the most profitable for the company owning the street, especially due to the huge mall that had opened less than two miles from here. Business was hard to come by, and investors were rare.

I'd managed to make three sales fall through, the last one thanks to Luca Montanari and his friendship with the buyer, Carter King.

But a few stores had closed their doors, too scared that a sale would happen and catch them off guard. We couldn't blame them for putting themselves first, it was our livelihood, but the store closures reduced foot traffic even more, and now that the sale had actually happened, I didn't think I could even do anything. But I had to try if only to be able to look at myself in the mirror, knowing I'd done everything I could.

At least all the agitation stopped me from stressing about entering a building that was owned by Sebastiano, and what would I even say to the person in charge of the deal?

I will offer them to let us renters buy the street, and then what?

I sighed, shaking my head. At least I was dressed more or less presentable today and wore my best pair of light blue jeans and a red shirt that wasn't stained yet. I even washed and brushed my hair this morning. Honestly, it was as dressed up as I was these days.

It didn't matter much anyway; they knew who they would meet. I wasn't a fancy CEO with a lot of money, or a rich heiress. I was a high-school graduate who inherited a business she had to fight for to keep a roof over her head and food on her table.

"Do you need anything?" I asked Becky, almost hoping she would say yes and prevent me from stepping even remotely into Sebastiano's universe.

She shook her head and made a shooing motion toward the door. "Go, go! This is much more important!"

I sighed and nodded again, grabbing the file with the basic business plan we'd put together when the landlord informed us of their intention of selling, one they had barely looked at, not that I could blame them. If I had been in their shoes with the only optic to make money, I would have probably laughed at us as well.

I rehearsed my speech in my head a few times as I took the subway to Manhattan and Montanari tower where it seems that Visconti was renting a floor.

Mafia sticks together. I thought bitterly, knowing that even if Gianluca Montanari listened to my plea once before he would not do it against one of *his* people.

As soon as I stepped into the fancy, expensive building, I regretted every single choice I'd made since finding this notice on my door. Starting with coming here dressed as I was. It looked perfectly acceptable in Indie Row and in my neighborhood but certainly not in this marble-clad reception with people dressed in the latest fashion while looking at me as if I was not worth the dirt under their shoes.

Way to go unnoticed, Calypso! I thought, but stood straight and raised my chin high, meeting their stares with my own.

They could judge me, but they were not better than me, than any of us. It was all the luck of a draw in life and some just got better cards.

I walked tall and proud to the reception desk and waited for the blonde woman behind it to be done with her call.

"Is it for a delivery of some sort?" she asked, her mouth slightly tipped down in disgust. "You're supposed to use the service entrance at the back." She pointed a perfectly manicured nail behind her. "You need to—"

"I'm here to meet a person in management at Visconti International."

She pursed her lips and started to type on her keyboard. "Name?"

"I don't have an appointment but—"

She sighed, pressing the button on her headset. "I can't let you up if you don't have an appointment." She looked behind me at the woman dressed nicely.

I moved to the side to block her line of vision. "Please, could you just call them and tell them that the representative of Indie Row would like to talk to them."

She opened her mouth, but I shook my head.

"I'm not leaving until you make the call to at least give them the opportunity to see me."

I heard a sigh from behind me and glanced at the woman who looked at her watch in irritation.

I shrugged. "Your call, but it seems that people are losing patience."

"You'll leave if I do that?"

I nodded.

She muttered something under her breath and typed a number on her phone before pressing the button of her headset again.

"Good morning, this is Melinda from the main reception," she said with a jovial voice, impressively hiding her level of irritation. "There is someone here for you, she said she's the representative of In—" She gave me a pointed look.

"Indie row." I reminded her.

"Indie Row," she repeated, the condescension so clear in her voice. "She would like to meet one of the managers." Her eyebrows arched as she listened to the person on the phone and turned toward me. "What's your name?"

"Caly Price."

She repeated my name to the person on the phone and after a few seconds; she turned to me with a slight shake of her head. "This name is not on their list. Miss, if—"

"It has to be I'm the representative. I'm Cal—" I stopped, they wouldn't be that cruel, were they? I sighed. "My full name is Calypso Price."

She arched an eyebrow, the corner of her mouth tipping up in a mocking smile, and I had to do my best not to roll my eyes. There was a reason why I never used my full name, and the woman in front of me was the perfect example. I was just lucky she wouldn't have the time or the desire to ask all the customary follow-up questions about the uniqueness of my name.

She repeated my name, and I didn't miss the little snort at the end of it. "Very well, yes, I will send her up immediately."

She reached into her drawer and retrieved a visitor badge. She swiped it and pointed at the webcam on top of her screen. "Look here. Okay, perfect." She typed on her keyboard for a few seconds and handed me the badge. "You must keep it on you at all times. Please swipe it when you step into the elevator. It will take you to the ninth floor."

"Thank you." I grabbed the badge and clipped it to my shirt. "You can do it, Caly," I whispered to myself as I reached the elevator.

It was already a good thing that they agreed to see me, right? Maybe they'd be happy to consider an alternative option. I tried to convince myself by taking deep breaths in.

The elevator opened to a long corridor with a few doors, and I followed the red arrow indicating Visconti to the right.

I had to admit it surprised me he didn't have the whole floor, but at the same time, Visconti's kingdom was Las Vegas. His business was just a guest in this town.

I pushed the glass door and as soon as I stepped in I saw the older woman behind a very basic desk. She pointed to the wide black door.

"Please go directly in. You only have a few minutes."

I took a deep breath and opened the door to find a spacious office with an office chair turned toward the bay window.

"Excuse me?" I called once the door closed behind me, only seeing the back of a dark-haired head. I twitched with discomfort, taking a couple more steps into the office. "Thank you for taking the time to see me. I'm Caly Price, Indie Row representative and—"

"What did I tell you about hiding your name, Calypso?"

My heart dipped in my chest when I heard the deep, gravely stentorian voice I'd not heard in six years.

He turned around on his seat, and I gripped the back of the leather chair in front of his desk to stop my legs from giving out.

Sebastiano Visconti was in front of me, his snarky smile on his face, his eyes reflecting his smugness as he detailed me with his dark brown eyes.

Sebastiano… My first love and my worst pain—The proof that love could be the cruelest thing you could experience and the reason why I kept every man I ever met at a reasonable distance since then, never daring to give any of them a shot to my heart.

Six years since he'd vanished and right now, I felt like it had been yesterday.

Chapter 2

Sebastiano

*C*alypso... A name impossible to forget just like the woman herself. I was not sure what to expect when I saw her in person again but that was not it.

It felt like all my nerves had awoken all at once as if she had a physical pull on me. I didn't miss the way she gripped the back of the seat in front of her.

I detailed her. She was even more beautiful than in my memory in an almost surreal way.

All I'd done in the past few weeks was to ensure she'd be standing here in front of me, and now that she was here, all I could do was stare at her.

She was not the innocent eighteen-year-old I'd left abandoned in her bed in the middle of the night. She was twenty-four now, and I could see that she'd filled out nicely—These few years apart had been generous to her. She was curvier, her breasts bigger... Her face was more defined, making her plump rosy lips even plumper than in my memory. Would they still taste as good? Would they be as soft? It was something I would need to check very soon. I had to stop myself from reaching up and touching my own lips at the memory.

"What are you doing here?" she asked, having infuriatingly recovered faster than I had. Her voice carried a wariness and a dash of coldness I couldn't blame her for.

What I did to her six years ago was far from kind, but I had my reasons no matter what she believed.

I looked up from her lustful lips to her angry bright aquamarine blue eyes that I knew were the reason for her unique name. She'd worn it as a stigma more than a badge of honor during her teenage years—That had been until she, unknowingly entered my world, and I'd made her mine with just one look not fully realizing at the time that, while I was busy making her mine, I was becoming hers too.

"What are you doing here, Sebastiano?" she asked again, dipping her fingers even deeper into the seat in front of her.

Her sultry voice calling my name caused my heart and dick to quiver with anticipation, and I wanted to hear her saying it repeatedly if possible while she was naked under me with my dick buried deep in her tight, hot heat.

"You're the one in my office, Calypso. My presence makes sense. *You're* the one coming to *me*," I added before gesturing to the seat she was grabbing for dear life in a silent invitation to sit.

She shook her head. "Aren't you above all this?" She gestured to the office. "This is a minor office in another man's territory. We both know you shouldn't be the one sitting in this chair."

I kept my face blank despite the surge of surprise this simple sentence caused. She mentioned territories, and that was not something people outside of our world really knew. She'd been so blissfully unaware of the mafia when I walked away yet she seemed to know more now. As for me sitting here, of course, it was beneath me, it was plainly ridiculous, but I was not a fool, and I knew that she'd not be standing here if she'd thought it was even a small possibility.

"You were hard to find. Price—" I cocked my head to the side. "What was wrong with Reynolds?"

"You're a smart businessman," she continued, completely ignoring my question. "What business do you have buying Indie Row? Even Gianluca didn't want it."

I pursed my lips, I hated that she spoke the name of another man, especially another capo, and the fact that Gianluca was a happy husband and father didn't matter. Calypso Reynolds belonged to one capo, and it was *me*.

"It got you here, didn't it." I didn't mean to say that, at least not yet, but she was frustrating me, and seeing the surprise on her face, opening and closing her mouth like a fish out of water made it worth it.

"You spent twelve million to get me to this office?"

Seventeen actually, but who's counting?

"I'm not sure your father would approve. Did you ask him before doing that?"

I frowned at the acid dripping from her taunting words. My Calypso had been sweet and kind. She didn't have any coldness or bite that this version seemed to have.

"My father is gone. I'm in charge."

"I'd like to give you my condolences, but I'm not big on theatrics."

I raised an eyebrow, not able to hide my surprise this time. "What happened to you?"

"You did." She sighed. "I can see that I've made a mistake coming here. Nothing good could come from this meeting. I'll apply via the appropriate channels to stop these forced closures. Indie Row is an institution, and it would take more than someone like you to scare me away."

I tried to ignore the effect her growing passion and heated cheeks did to my body. That was something that at least remained the same. She was still passionate.

"Why do you want to save that old obsolete street?" I asked, cocking my head to the side. "Most of these businesses can barely pay their rent, and I know for a fact the old woman beside yours has been paying the same rent since 1970, and even that she can't do!"

"You're not losing any money from her store. We've been paying the gap in her rent."

"Don't you—" I sighed. I enjoyed her passion but not when it was going against my interests. "You can see this market is not viable! The whole thing is falling apart." I pointed at the window behind me. "Since the highway was extended and the train lines changed, the foot traffic in that street was reduced by sixty-eight percent."

"And yet you spent the money, you must see the potential. You're shrewd and calculating," she spat.

To get to you, to have you in the palm of my hand. I wanted to retort. *You are worth 17 million and only you.*

"You say that as if they're flaws, they are positive qualities to me." I pointed to her and then to me. "This is what makes the difference between me sitting here in my designer suit with *billions* in my accounts and you, standing in front of me, dressed in Target's latest fashion with an account in overdraft."

She pursed her lips and took a step back. "I'm done here. You'll never understand, and I don't care enough to explain things to you. Indie Row is an institution. I'll find a few local councilors ready to listen to me and we'll lobby against these forceful, unfair, evictions. We won't go down without a fight."

"And for each councilor who listens, you'll find I'll have two more powerful ones in my pocket, but please... be my guest," I taunted, gesturing toward the door, calling her bluff.

However, once again, she took me by surprise when she turned around and stormed toward it. Fuck, this silly woman was ready to go into a fight she was certain to lose.

"I'll give it to you," I shouted reluctantly as her hand touched the handle. She was making me reveal my plan a lot faster than I'd anticipated.

She stopped and turned her head to the side. "What?"

I sighed. "You heard me."

She turned around slowly but stayed by the door. "You'll *give* it to me?"

I nodded once.

She took a couple of wary steps forward, her eyes shrouded in doubt.

"You will give me Indie Row? Something worth twelve million, no strings attached?"

"Seventeen actually, and yes, I'll transfer the deed to you. I never said it was without conditions though."

She let out a humorless laugh. "Whatever you're offering I'm not interested." She shook her head. "Been there, done that, got the T-shirt to prove it."

Once again, she was not acting like I had planned, forcing me to rethink my whole strategy on the spot.

"Why are you so difficult?" I let out, not able to conceal my exasperation as well as I wanted to.

"I'm not difficult, I'm strong. I know my worth now."

"You know you won't win a war against me. You know that, don't you?"

"Why? Because you're mafia?" She shrugged. "Nothing is stopping me from trying."

I froze. "Mafia?"

She rolled her eyes. "We're way past that."

I would find out who told her, and I would take my time breaking every bone in his body. "So, you wouldn't even consider whatever I have to offer out of spite? Knowing full well you'll lose whatever battle you'll start and put those poor people out of business, including your old and sick elderly neighbor."

She pursed her lips and crossed her arms on her chest. It was a defensive pose, but the way it raised her full breasts was delicious.

"What do you want?"

Here you are... I stopped myself from smiling as she finally took the bait.

"Come back with me to Las Vegas."

She looked at me for a couple of seconds, blinking fast before bursting into laughter.

This morphed my previous annoyance into full anger. Anyone else who dared laugh at me the way she was would have a bullet in their body already.

I slammed my hand on the desk. "Do not laugh at me, Calypso!" I roared.

She stopped immediately, and I hated the fear I saw flash on her face. I regretted losing my cool with her, I never wanted her to fear me.

"I'm sorry." She sobered up and wiped at the tears under her eyes. "You have to be joking if you think there's even the slightest chance for me to go anywhere with you."

I had to use all my willpower not to snap at her again and took a deep breath. "Fina is getting married next weekend. I want you to come with me."

"Ah," She nodded, her face softening and carrying a sadness I didn't truly expect.

She'd been the one breaking my sister's heart when she just vanished, never responding to her call or text and cutting her best friend out of her life without an explanation.

Like you did to her? The voice in my head taunted.

"I wish Serafina the best, I truly do, and I hope it is a marriage born from love, not obligations."

"It is," I confirmed, realizing she knew a lot more than I gave her credit for.

"Then I'm genuinely happy for her, but I'm not going there."

"Even for seventeen million?"

"Even for all the richness of the world."

"Damn." I leaned back on my seat with a little laugh that I hoped would cover the sting of such a blatant rejection. "What are you offering?"

"In exchange for the street?"

I nodded.

"My eternal gratitude?" she said it with a tone that was all but truthful.

I leaned my elbows on my desk and let my eyes trail up slowly from her sneakers; up her body stopping at all the places I'd like to kiss, lick or penetrate until I reached her eyes and licked my bottom lip at her flustered face, clearly knowing what I was after. "No."

"I don't sleep with married men," she let out in a breath, visibly affected by the erotic moment we just shared.

"Is it where you draw the line? That's a pretty low bar." I mocked but suddenly wondered how many men had the chance to touch her the way I was the first to do, and I hated them all, wanting to wipe them from the face of this earth, so no one alive would know the feeling of getting lost in her arms. I also wondered why she thought I was married. It wasn't a crazy assumption, mind you. I was approaching thirty, insanely rich, and I had the looks and dick to match.

She shrugged, tilting her chin up in challenge.

Oh, my sweet Calypso, I'm going to eat you whole.

"Good," I showed her my left hand, bare of any ring. "Because I'm not married."

She jerked back in surprise. "Ah she left you, I'm sorry. Divorce must suck."

"Who left me? I'm not divorced, I was never married. Who was I supposed to marry?"

She opened her mouth and closed it again before shaking her head as if she was having an internal debate.

"What do you want? To sleep with me?"

I remained silent, keeping my eyes locked with hers.

"I'll give you one night."

My dick hardened at the thought of having her again, and I was grateful that my desk hid the extent of my arousal. "Do you think a night with you is worth that much?"

She shook her head. "No, but based on the way you're acting, you do."

Who was the calculating one now?

"You would be selling yourself to me? You wouldn't be more than a glorified prostitute."

"I know."

"You've changed."

"I have, and you already took what I had to give, so it wouldn't matter much."

I'll make it matter. I was going to make sure that once she was in my bed again, she would never leave it, but I needed to make certain of that.

"Three nights, and I'll do whatever I want to you."

She looked down, but I didn't miss the blush. She was still my sweet innocent Calypso under all this bravado.

She shook her head again. "No, it's one night or nothing."

"To do whatever I want?"

"Will you give me the title then?"

"I'll get the papers done right now, and I'll give them to you then and there."

She hesitated before nodding and my dick got so hard at the thought of what I could do to her that it was painful.

"Tonight, my hotel room."

"No, I've got plans tonight."

My nostrils flared at the thought of her having plans with anyone but me. "No, tonight." I commended. "I'm staying at the Ritz-Carlton. Central Park Suite." I reached into my pocket and got out my card key, sliding it on my desk. "Be there at 8 p.m."

She looked at the golden card and shook her head. "Not your room, not your hotel."

"Why not?"

"Because I have another condition."

I sighed. "You have a lot of those... Let's hear it."

"After tonight and whatever you do to my body, I want you to do exactly as you did six years ago." She locked eyes with me and the determination I saw there impressed me. "I want to wake up alone in a cold bed. I want you to be gone, and I never want to hear from you again."

I had to admit that no matter how ready I thought I'd been this rejection touched a part of me that no one but her could reach, even six years later.

"St. Regis Hotel, 8 p.m.," I offered through gritted teeth. That was my last concession. One more thing and I'll just drug her and take her on my fucking plane.

She nodded. "I'll be there. Don't forget the papers," she added before swirling around and leaving this office, and I didn't stop it this time.

I stood up once she was gone and walked to the reception. "You can go back to your actual job," I told Gianluca's assistant who was sitting behind the desk. "Tell Gianluca thank you for me."

"I will do, Mr. Visconti. Happy to help."

I sighed leaning against the threshold as the woman left. These offices didn't exist, not really, it was just a dummy address to have her come to me.

You were mine once, Calypso Reynolds, you'll be mine again, I vowed as I walked back into the office to grab my laptop and start phase B of my plan.

Chapter 3

Caly

I looked at the clock on the wall as I entered my apartment. It was already 6:30 p.m. and the bus ride from the East Bronx to his stupid fancy hotel will take me about an hour.

It took me quite some time to reassure people from Indie Row, telling them that we might reach a deal tomorrow, and then I had to reorganize my whole evening at such short notice which was always a challenge for someone in my situation.

I wanted to cancel, I should do it. Sebastiano broke my heart and flipped my whole life upside down.

I'd not been with a man since him, somehow scared of letting a man touch me again. This one time with him had dear consequences, something that I would pay until the end of my life. How could I go through all this again? How could I ever be with him again?

Just seeing him all-powerful and masculine today made me feel all the things I thought were dead. I was confused about all the things he told me; were they lies? I still had the wedding invitation in my box of painful memories. The one I still opened every once in a while, when I felt guilty about some of the choices I'd made.

I jumped into the shower and scrubbed the day away knowing that no matter how much of a mistake it was, I was not the only one to consider in this decision. I had responsibilities and commitments I could not shy away from.

I got out of the shower, and as I rushed around to slip into my bathrobe I dropped all the bottles on the counter at the same time and cursed what was about to follow.

I had barely walked into the kitchen when I heard a knock on the door. I sighed looking heavenward, I could not catch a break.

"I'm sorry, Mrs. Newman," I called, reaching the door. "I didn't mean to—" I stopped when I opened the door to find Sebastiano standing in the small corridor of my building.

He was not in his fancy suit anymore but in a pair of dark jeans and a pale blue polo shirt, his hair slicked back as he used to do when we were younger. This version of Sebastiano was much closer to the one who left me behind, but he was more manly, wider, radiating the power and responsibilities he now carried.

"Sebastiano." I pulled the door closer to me. "What are you doing here?"

He smiled, raising his hand and showing me the bag he held. "I brought food. Best Thai in the city. Do you still have a soft spot for Thai green curry?"

"You're not supposed to be here."

He pursed his lips, his good humor vanishing. "Why? Is anyone there?" He moved to look over my head. "Is your boyfriend in there?" He took a step forward, and I held the door tighter against my body.

He looked down at me, his scowl now chilling. "Does he know all the filthy stuff I'm going to do to you? Is he okay to sell you for seventeen million dollars?"

"You sold me for a lot less," I replied before I could stop myself. I sighed. "Nobody is here, it's only me, but I don't want you in my space."

"Tonight is mine to do as I wish, and I wish to have dinner with you at your place." He raised his other hand showing me the folder he held. "These are the documents, let me in now, or lose this."

I could feel my heart in my throat with apprehension at the idea of having him here. The risk of him discovering the truth was too great. I was not sure things were safe.

"Just give me a few minutes, I'm not dressed for company." I pointed to my robe and bare feet.

"Actually, you're dressed exactly as you should be for *my* company." He took another step closer. So close that the tip of his shoes brushed my bare toes. "Let. Me. In. Calypso" He ordered through gritted teeth.

I looked inside my apartment for a few seconds, scanning the small room as fast as possible hoping that any evidence of my secret was hidden from plain sight.

I sighed, letting go of the door.

He pushed it open and stormed in as if he owned the place, which in his head he probably did.

For seventeen million, he can. My conscience reminded me.

He looked around the room silently before turning toward me. "It's tiny."

"We can't all be billionaires," I retorted, closing the door behind him. "And you're six foot three, everything is tiny for you."

"Six foot four, but who's counting," he replied, turning toward the kitchen counter and putting the food there.

"You do, always, money has always been the way you talk," I replied before sighing and jerking my head toward his shoes. "Shoes off."

He removed his shoes, keeping his eyes on me. "Yes, I remember how you disapproved of my vision of the world."

"Money can't buy everything," I replied, still a firm believer in this.

He let out a little laugh as he opened the bag and put all the food containers on the counter, there was too much for two.

"Money can't buy everything and yet here you are, about to submit," he said tauntingly.

That one stung deep because it was true, I was selling myself, and it didn't matter if it was for twenty dollars or seventeen million. I was not sure it was something I could ever fully recover from.

I looked down, blinking my tears away.

"Calypso," he started, and I hated the softness of his voice.

"Can I see the papers?" I asked, raising my head, trying to take the same cool facade I'd seen him wear so many times. "It's nothing more than a business transaction after all"

He scowled again as if he hated being reminded of the fact. "Don't you trust me?"

I couldn't help but laugh at that. "Excuse me if I don't."

He sighed and extended the documents toward me. I looked through them, pretending to know what I was looking for but except for my name on an ownership deed I was not even sure was legal, nothing else made sense.

"I'll be right back," I replied, going into my bedroom to hide the papers in my safe, in other words, under my mattress, and hiding the two picture frames I had there before walking back into the main room and finding him sitting at my counter, ready to eat as if he belonged here.

"Come." He jerked his head to the bar stool beside him. "Let's eat before the food gets cold."

I stayed where I was, knowing that giving my body to him again was already so difficult, but the idea of sharing a meal, chatting, and being intimate in this way seemed almost too much to bear.

Sebastiano always had the ability to see right through me before, and I feared what he could uncover now.

"You don't need to seduce me," I said with a mocking tone. "I'm all paid for."

His jaw clenched, and his nostrils flared. "Yes, I paid for the fucking evening, and right now I want to eat and talk." He jerked his head toward the seat again. "Sit your *fucking* ass down, Calypso," he barked, and I couldn't remember even hearing him swear at me like that before.

I needed to remember that he was not the young man he once was. He had changed just like I had. He was a mafia boss now and had been for quite some time. The softness I'd thought I saw so many years ago was obviously gone... if it'd ever existed at all.

That jerked me into action as I took the seat beside him, looking at the name of the restaurant printed on the takeaway box. That was the Thai everybody was raving about online in the heart of Manhattan and where I could never justify spending that much money.

He pushed one container toward me. "Eat. You still love Thai green curry, right? It used to be your favorite."

I nodded mutedly and grabbed the fancy pair of chopsticks.

I took a few bites in silence, marveling at the taste but being petty enough not to tell him.

"So, tell me, what happened to you?" he asked after taking a couple of bites as well.

"I'm not sure I understand."

"When I left you in Vegas, you were a month away from your high school graduation with a full scholarship to study hospitality management at UNLV, and now you're here living in the Bronx owning an old, obsolete, and dying bakery."

I remembered the girl I used to be, full of big dreams. The ones he used to listen to when we'd talk about managing a big Vegas Casino one day.

"Thank you for giving me a rundown of my life—Just in case I forgot."

"What happened?" he asked again, ignoring my sarcasm.

You happened. I shrugged. "I'm not sure what the answer is to that. It was just silly dreams, one of many; life happened."

"Your mother moved to Reno after your father died three years ago, and she remarried. How come you don't talk anymore?"

I shouldn't have been surprised that he knew everything about my life and family, which made it even more necessary for me to get rid of him.

I put the chopsticks back on the table and looked at him.

"What do you want to hear me say?"

His eyes dipped down and stopped, taking a sensual hue I could hardly forget, and that still made my lower stomach squeeze uncomfortably.

I followed his eyes and saw that my robe had opened, probably when I shrugged, revealing one of my erect nipples.

"Don't!" he ordered as I reached to the side to close the robe.

He licked his lips, his eyes on my nipple, and licked them again, making it harden to the point of pain.

"Will they taste as good as in my memory?" he asked, his voice much huskier now.

When I remained silent, he stood up and closed the distance between us before reaching for my waist and spinning me on my seat, so he could squeeze his way between my legs.

He let his fingers run on the side of my neck, causing my whole body to shiver, and grabbed the robe down to one side and then the other until it was at my waist.

He kept his eyes on my chest as he let his fingers run down it, and he cupped my right breast.

"They are larger than in my memory," he said in a low voice, clearly talking to himself. He started to knead it gently, and I gasped as he reached for my nipple, pinching it between his fingers as arousal soaked my panties.

I closed my eyes, hating the way I was responding to his touch, his voice, his whole presence.

How could I still want him that much? Maybe I needed closure, maybe I needed to know this time was the last and not get consumed with a future we would never have, like I did last time.

I let out a low moan as I felt his warm tongue lap at my exposed nipple.

"Ummm, even better," he whispered against my sensitive skin, and I opened my eyes wide as he sucked it into his mouth.

He swirled his tongue around it, and I couldn't stop myself from burying my hand in his thick black hair.

He let my nipple out of his mouth with a loud pop before concentrating on the other.

I rocked on my seat, my body taking over and seeking a satisfaction I didn't know I was craving so much. I rocked again and this time he pulled me toward him, and I had no other choice but to wrap my legs around his waist as my heated core pressed against the hard ridges of his throbbing erection.

He rested his hands under my ass and turned to walk me into the bedroom. He had a wild look in his eyes as he looked down at me, which made my lower belly squeeze painfully in anticipation.

His eyes locked with my lips, and he leaned down. It took a couple of seconds for my lust-filled brain to understand his intentions, and I turned my head just before his lips connected with mine, landing on the corner instead.

"Calypso..." he trailed off—his tone unmistakably warning me.

He laid me on the bed and stayed between my opened legs, moving his hips rhythmically, brushing his hardness against my soaked panties, giving my clitoris such delicious friction I was on the verge of orgasm.

I gasped, raising my hips to meet his, trying to increase the friction.

"Calypso, look at me." And when I did, he leaned down again, and I turned my head again avoiding his kiss.

He groaned with frustration, letting his teeth graze my jawline, and I whined as he stopped the delicious movement of his hips.

He grabbed my jaw between his fingers, not hard enough to bruise but enough to restrict my ability to move it. "Don't fight me on this, Calypso. I want to kiss you, and I will."

I knew it was stupid with what we were about to do and how intimate my body would be with his in a few minutes, but I was partial to his kisses, this was how I had become addicted to him, how I had been lost in him, and I was too scared to not resist him. I would much rather suck on his dick. It was something he'd taught me when we had started to explore and something I had really enjoyed at the time.

"No, Sebastiano, please. Don't kiss me," I begged.

"On the mouth?"

"Yes?" I replied with a questioning tone, not sure I knew what he even meant by that.

His face morphed into a wicked smile, and I knew I just fell into whatever trap he set for me.

He kissed my chin and went down, peppering my neck with little kisses until he reached my breast and gave both nipples a long, hard lick. He stood up, untying the belt of my robe and pulling down my white cotton panties in the same breath, not even giving me the time to feel embarrassed.

He stood at the bottom of the bed, staring at my naked body that was dimly lit by the main room light and the streetlight.

His dark, intense eyes made me self-conscious, and I felt my skin heat up under his unwavering eyes.

A side smile spread on his lips. "Your body is still mine, *naiade mia,* even if you seem to have forgotten who you belong to."

He pulled up his shirt and threw it on the floor. "Spread your legs for me."

I kept them closed as I stared at his magnificent chest now covered with strong muscles and a few more tattoos than when I'd known him.

"Your legs, Calypso," he commanded, his voice carrying the underlying threat. "You're mine to do what I want with, remember? Don't make me call my lawyer to cancel the deal." He unbuckled his belt. "Spread them wide for me. Let me see what's mine."

"For the evening," I replied, bending my knees and spreading my legs open as far as they could go, opening myself unbashful, showing him the extent of my wetness and need for him.

"*Quello che vuoi.*" He licked his lips, keeping his eyes on my pussy as he unzipped his pants and took them down with his boxers, revealing his long hard cock that got me tongue-tied as it did every time I saw it.

He kneeled on the floor and grabbed my legs making me shriek in surprise as he pulled me to the edge.

"Time for my favorite meal, wet nymph".

I gasped and arched my back with the first long, hard swipe of his tongue on my slit. It had been so long; I'd forgotten how good it felt to be worshiped that way even if it wasn't born from love as I'd thought when I was young but out of basic lust.

"Oh god!" I whimpered, grabbing at my quilt instead of reaching for his hair.

His lapping turned more forceful, more insistent, before he pushed two fingers inside me.

"So tight," he growled against my clit, the vibration sending an electrical current up my spine. He sucked at my clit as his fingers started a slow deep back and forth inside me, and I felt my walls tighten around them as my body looked for the orgasm that was maddening close.

"More. More. Sebastiano, please."

"Say you're mine," he asked, never raising his head from between my legs.

I shook my head from side to side. "No, I can't."

He increased the pace of his fingers, sucking at my clit again, and as my walls clamped on his fingers at the orgasm building at the base of my spine he stopped abruptly.

"Let me kiss you if you want to come... Tell me I can kiss you."

"I—yes, yes you can. Kiss me!"

He sucked on my clit hard and pushed his fingers firmly inside me, and I came so hard, I saw a flash of light.

He pushed me back on the bed and settled on top of me, crashing his wet lips on mine, invading my mouth with his skillful tongue that tasted like me. It was erotic and almost obscene all at once, and I let his devouring possession swallow me whole as he dominated me with his tongue.

He brushed his cock against my slit a couple of times, never breaking the kiss and pushed to the hilt in one powerful thrust.

I couldn't contain the cry of pain at the invasion because despite my wetness and preparation it had been six years since I had sex, and I only had it once before. He was big, really big, and his roughness felt like it split me in two.

He raised on his elbows, looking down at me with a confused frown on his face. "Calypso?"

I shook my head, blinking back the tears. "It's fine; keep on going."

He stayed in me, unmoving for a few more seconds, scanning my face as if he was looking for some answers.

I grabbed his face and pulled him down for a kiss, anything to break his close examination of me.

He kissed me gently as he started to move slowly, and my heart broke in my chest because it felt like the first time he made love to me in the hotel room at The Mirage. It was gentle and pleasurable. It was not the rough fucking he had prepared me for, but he felt like he was making love to me, and I could almost believe what I believed so many years ago; that he loved me.

After a few moments, his speed and force increased as he whispered things in Italian that I couldn't understand.

I felt the orgasm build again and as his thrusts turned erratic; he reached between our bodies and rubbed at my clit, making me come again as my walls tightened around him. He groaned and kissed me deeply as he emptied himself in me.

He rolled away, and I didn't get a chance to move away as he grabbed me around the waist and pulled me to his chest.

"No, you're still mine for a few hours," he said with a sleepy voice. "Sleep now," he ordered, keeping me locked against his body, and against all odds I did, soothed by the soft thuds of his heart.

***

When I woke up, I was satisfied, sore, and alone.

I sighed and lay on my back, feeling sadness despite the fact that his disappearance was my condition. Sleeping with him had been a mistake, no matter what string was attached. It had reopened all the wounds I'd thought were healed, and I knew I would have to grieve us all over again.

This cruel love had still an—I jerked to a sitting position as I heard a loud banging sound in the kitchen.

I grabbed my robe from the floor and wrapped it around me, before tightening my hair in a messy bun and walked to the kitchen to find Sebastiano wearing only his blue jeans, cooking eggs.

Panic started to set in. He was supposed to be gone. He needed to be.

"What are you still doing here?" I asked, looking at the clock. I barely had a couple of hours.

He threw me a side look before looking back at his pan. "I changed my mind."

"You—" I shook my head. "No, it was a one-night thing."

He sighed, removed the pan from the heat, and turned toward me. "It's not enough. I want more. I want all of you."

I shook my head as anxiety, and want battled inside me. Maybe if my life was different, I could indulge in a few more days with him no matter how much it would hurt once he walked away, but I had to protect my secret at all costs.

"No, you have to leave now." I pointed to his chest. "You don't belong in my life."

He took a step toward me, and as he opened his mouth to speak my worst nightmare happened.

I heard the unmistakable sound of a key sliding into the lock and the instant fear I felt froze me on the spot.

It was over, it was all over, I thought as the door opened and the love of my life ran like a little ball of energy while Sarah apologized profusely for being early.

"Mommy! We can't be late to the zoo and—" He stopped, facing Sebastiano sporting a scowl that made him the carbon copy of the man standing, frozen in shock, the spatula in his fist.

"Who are you?" he asked Sebastiano, the command in his voice surprisingly similar.

The worst case scenario had happened—Damion was standing face to face with his father, and there was nothing I could do.

Chapter 4

Sebastiano

I blinked at the tiny little boy standing in front of me, my ears buzzing, and my heart lost somewhere in the depths of my stomach.

Mine! My mind screamed, trying to shake me out of my stupor. That boy was mine, there was no question, no possible doubt. He was my spitting image up to the small mole under his left eye. He was me, except for Calypso's mesmerizing eyes.

"Damion, go to your room and get ready for the zoo. Also, Ms. Daniels sent me a message about your drawing..."

I looked at the little boy give her a cheeky smile that made my heart squeeze and followed him with my eyes to his bedroom.

"Oh, I'm sorry—I didn't..." the other woman stuttered.

I followed the boy, *my* boy to his bedroom as Calypso hurried the other woman out.

I looked around the room and a heavy weight settled in the pit of my stomach. Her bedroom had been ridiculously sparse, but this little boy had everything, including a bed shaped like a car.

He put his backpack on his desk and turned to me.

"Why are you here? Are you a friend of mommy? Where is your shirt? Are you coming to the zoo with Jeremy and Mommy?"

I was not ready for the barrage of questions and inquisitive eyes on me. I was actually not familiar with children at all come to think of it.

"Oh, ummm, yes, my name is Sebastiano, and I'm a friend of your mom, and I came this morning because I'm..." I stopped to think for a second. "Because Jeremy can't come, so I'm coming to the zoo too, and I stained my shirt."

I didn't know who the fuck Jeremy was, but there was no way he got to be close to my family.

My family... the thought took my breath away by how true it felt, and I couldn't help but sit down on his bed, feeling like a misplaced giant.

I wanted this family despite the anger I felt against the woman in the other room. I'd come back to make Calypso mine again, maybe that was destiny after all.

"Ah." He nodded as if it made sense. "Did you eat coco puffs? I always stain my shirt when I eat them, but Mommy is good at cleaning it. You will be okay."

I smiled, a little too overwhelmed by emotions to speak, and I looked at him emptying his bag and babbling about what activity he would do at the zoo.

"Sebastiano?"

I blinked a couple of times and turned toward Calypso who was now dressed in sweatpants and a T-shirt, holding my shirt in her hand.

"Oh, you cleaned the stain?" Damion asked her with a smile before turning toward me, the cheeky light in his blue eyes reminded me of my sweet young Calypso. "See I told you Mommy could clean everything."

"It's not a reason to always make it hard for me," she chastised him with good humor. "You can go now," she said to me. "I'm sorry but we have a busy day."

This forceful rejection, coupled with her deception caused my anger to multiply, and I could feel the hot coil in my chest burn as never before.

I stood up briskly, causing her to take a step back. The look I gave her was enough to make her pale, but I was too angry to care right now.

"I thought Sebastiano was coming with us," Damion asked, confused.

"Sebastiano is coming," I replied, keeping my eyes on Calypso and giving her the most chilling stare I had. The one I reserved for people I was on the verge of killing. I guess I could also give it to the woman I was about to kidnap and never let go.

I saw all the signs of fear in her, the swallowing, the increased speed in her breathing and once again I didn't care.

"Why don't you finish your drawing for Ms. Daniels now."

"But Moooommmy," he whined.

"You know the rule, Damion," she said sternly.

Fuck I loved that strict mother side of her. *No, Sebastiano don't go there, she wronged you!* My voice of reason chimed trying to smother the voice of my dick.

He sighed. "Okay, sorry mommy."

I followed her outside the room, and as soon as she closed the door I gripped her upper arm hard enough to make her gasp and maybe even bruise and pulled her to the other side of the room, way too angry to care about leaving my marks on her skin in anything other than pleasure.

"This boy is *mine*," I whispered angrily keeping my hold on her arm.

"No, he is *mine*." She tried to shake my hold, but I tightened it making her wince. "He's been mine for six years. I'm the one who gave birth to him, who fed him, changed his diapers, kept him safe." She blinked back tears, and I loosened my hold ever so slightly because no matter how angry I was, causing her pain didn't sit well with me.

I leaned closer to her, my nose almost touching hers. "And who's fault is that, huh?" I asked through gritted teeth. "Is that why you wanted me to stay away? Would you ever have told me?"

"No, never. I've learned my lesson," she replied, keeping her eyes locked with mine. "You can leave now, we'll never bother you, I swear."

I couldn't help but laugh at the absurdity of her words, as if there was a chance in the world I'd walk away from my blood, from something that she and I created in an act of love, no matter how much she'd deny it.

"You know what's going to happen, Calypso Reynolds?"

"Price," she corrected me.

"Reynolds," I insisted coldly. "You're going to take your phone, call that Jeremy and tell him to never ever come near you again."

She opened her mouth to reply, and I snapped, not ready to hear whatever she would say about the man. I crashed my lips on hers, kissing her with all the turmoil I felt because of hers.

I broke the kiss and she swayed, resting my hand on my bare chest to stay upright.

The feeling of her hand on my skin felt like a branding.

I grabbed her wrist and removed her hand. "Calypso!" I called, and she looked up to me, apprehension now replacing her previous bravado.

"We're going to take our son to the zoo, and you're going to pack a bag for both of you and jump in my jet tonight for Vegas."

"No." She shook her head vigorously. "Absolutely not, our life is here."

"Here?" I looked around with a mocking sneer. "Here in the Bronx? In a crappy apartment that's the size of my bedroom? You think you can raise the future capo of the Vegas Mafia in such a state?"

She paled again. "No, Damion is not—No." She shook her head again. "Sebastiano, everything, but not that."

I pulled her into her bedroom and closed the door behind us. "Look at this place!" I pointed to her bed, which was nothing more than a mattress on painted wooden pallets. "Look at your dying bakery! I'm sure he's going to a lame under-funded school with books dating from your grandmother's time! Is that the life you want for him? For you?" I grabbed her shoulders and shook her. "Is it better than a life of luxury with me in Vegas, where you could have all the best things money can buy?"

She pursed her lips, and I saw it, the cold hard truth that hurt me a lot more than I would have thought, and that ignited the petty desire to hurt her just as much. She'd rather live in misery than with me.

"Listen to me well. I'll take Damion to Vegas with or without you."

Liar, it was with her, willing or unconscious.

She took a step back, looking at me with weariness. "You can't, he's my son. I'll go to the police!"

I laughed, taking a step toward her which she mirrored, her back hitting the wall. "Sweetheart, you know who I am," I said, sounding as condescending as I could. "I own every fucking cop and every fucking judge. I'll get full custody of the boy before morning if I want to." I took another step toward her. "Do. Not. Test. Me. I have no qualms about taking him from you and letting you rot here."

She let out a tearless sob and rested a shaky hand on her lips. It hurt me that she believed I could do that. The old Calypso would never believe that I would treat her that way.

"He's everything to me."

"Then come, nothing is stopping you."

"What about Indie Row? Damion's school?"

"Not negotiable. Damion and you, or Damion alone."

"Why are you doing this?" she asked, her voice cracking, and I almost gave in when faced with her distress... Almost.

"Don't act like the victim, like *I'm* the bad guy. You wronged me—Now it's time to take back what's mine."

"Your son, is that it?"

"Yes." I grabbed the shirt from her hand. "My son. Now get ready, we have a zoo to go to."

My son and you, Calypso Reynolds. I'm taking back the family that should have been mine six years ago, I thought, exiting her room and closing the door behind me before I fell, powerless when confronted with her pain and distress.

Chapter 5

Caly

I pretended to smile, faced with Damion's excitement as we reached the tarmac and stopped close to the plane.

The trip to the zoo had been heartbreaking in so many ways—especially because of how well it went.

Damion connected immediately with Sebastiano as if his soul recognized his father somehow, and Sebastiano had been a completely different man as well. Caring, gentle... Part of me almost felt guilty for lying to Damion. Almost because then I remembered why I ran all the way to New York to live with a great-aunt I barely knew and then the anger at the dangerous man waiting on the plane started again.

I grabbed my sports bag as the silent driver opened the trunk to get out our two suitcases. I was not completely defeated yet. I hoped there'd be a chance for Sebastiano to let us go. He had been fickle then, and I was sure he was still like that now.

Having a child probably sounded like fun for him, but it was hard work and commitment, and I painfully experienced how Sebastiano viewed that.

I sighed as I extended my hand to Damion. "Remember what we said?"

He bounced with excitement but nodded quickly. "Always stay with you."

I looked down at him one more time as we reached the steps to the plane before straightening my back and walking up.

Sebastiano was sitting in the first row of luxury cream leather seats with a glass of scotch in his hand and a laptop open on the small table in front of him.

I met his eyes with the same unwavering look he was giving me, hoping that mine carried the contempt I felt.

"Is this plane yours?" Damion asked, breaking the staring contest.

Sebastiano looked down at him, his face softening. "Yes, all mine."

"Wow!" Damion looked around the plane in awe. "You're like batman rich!"

I couldn't help but laugh at that despite the bad situation, but I sobered quickly when I looked up and saw that Sebastiano was now looking at me with a knowing smile and a tenderness in his eyes that had no business being directed at me.

I shook my head and pulled Damion to the seats a few rows behind Sebastiano. I knew full well it was childish because we would be locked in this metal prison together for over five hours and the same once we reached Vegas, but I'd sworn to myself to take any type of distance I could, every chance I got.

I helped Damion to his seat and secured his seatbelt before opening my bag to retrieve the small grey box I had there. A box

I used to open daily when I was pregnant and in the first year of Damion's life but that rarely made an appearance now.

I called it the '*Cruel Love*' box—Something to remind me why I had made the choices I'd made, why I became the person I was, but when Aunt Millie died, it came with the realization that I had to move on and to do that I didn't need closure, an apology, or even for any of the people who caused me so much pain to acknowledge it.

But at the same time, I hated that he felt entitled to play the victim. The poor father deprived of his son. It may have been true that I had never shared my pregnancy with him, but it was not for lack of trying. He could see himself as a victim if he wanted to but he also needed to remember that he was the reason for it all.

I retrieved a notebook from the bag and colored pencils and placed them on the table in front of Damion. "I'll be right back, bunny. Just start making the list of everything you want to see."

I walked to Sebastiano's seat, and he moved the folders he'd put on his seat as an invitation to sit. As if.

I shook my head briskly. "It will only take a minute."

He sighed as if I was being unreasonable. "Sit down Calypso, we'll be taking off soon." He gestured to the air hostess who was preparing things on a tray. "Do you want something to drink?"

I looked at the hostess and smiled at her, she didn't deserve animosity, she had no play in this. "No thank you, I have drinks in my bags."

She gave me a tight smile and went back to her task.

"Calypso..." He let out a weary sigh and once again I hated how he was making me feel unreasonable when he was the one who was destroying my life... *again*!

He let his eyes trail down to the box in my hands. "What is that?"

I set the box on the table beside him and tapped on the lid. "This is just to refresh your memory as you seem to think you're the victim in this whole ordeal."

He looked up from the box with a raised eyebrow. "You think you are?"

I smiled at that. "Not anymore, not for a long time."

"You're the one who's living her best life, dating loser bankers, and voluntarily lied to me every chance you had since you walked into my office."

I leaned down and sneered. "You don't get to judge how *I* repaired what *you* destroyed." I pushed the box toward him. "Have a lovely trip down memory lane, Sebastiano Visconti," I told him before going back to my seat and doing my best to pretend to have the best time with Damion knowing that it was probably the most exciting day of his life.

It was already getting late when we got on the plane and all the excitement of the day got the better of Damion about an hour into the flight.

I reclined his seat and waved at the hostess to request a pillow and a blanket. I was only half surprised not to see Sebastiano turn his head to look at what I wanted. He still had his head bowed down, probably still looking at the contents of the box.

I sighed and leaned back in my own seat, closing my eyes and trying to relax a bit.

There was no reason for him to look at that box for so long. I knew by heart everything that was in it. Every memento, every word. There was my old phone that I took the time to charge back up tonight before leaving, so he could see how pathetic I had been after his departure. How many texts I sent him that remained unanswered, texts where I begged him to call me back as I had important news, each text being more desperate than the last.

I stopped when Visconti's father let me into his home one day, probably fed up to see the crying girl in front of the gates. He'd told me the truth about who they were, and I had felt betrayed not only by Sebastiano who lulled me into a relationship that had no future because how could you be with a man who hides who he was, but I also felt betrayed by Serafina who, as my best friend, should have told me why she had not approved of my attraction to her older brother.

Visconti senior had then given me a wedding invitation, one that was now in the box, wrinkled by my fists and tears. A wedding set in Parma for when I'd be seven months pregnant, I'd calculated quickly. A wedding between Sebastiano Maurizio Visconti Jr. and Annalucia Moretti—a woman I didn't know and hated on principle.

The last nail in my coffin had been the letter I'd received a week later, written in Sebastiano's recognizable handwriting.

I tightened my eyes closed, trying to prevent the tears from coming even six years later. I'd read this letter way too many times. I knew every word and replaying them now still caused me pain.

Calypso,

Nymph of the seven seas. I am sorry I have to write this letter, but my father informed me of your constant visits to our home. I thought my silence and my refusal to answer messages would have been clear as to the state of our so-called "relationship".

I'm sorry you misunderstood the nature of our fling and took it for something a lot more serious than it was.

It was always something light for me; there was no future between you and me. Surely if you're honest with yourself you know that too. I'm a legacy, born to rule over this city, and you are... Well, you are nice and sweet but outside of my world.

I'm sorry if your assumptions hurt you, and I truly wish you the best for the future.

Sebastiano.

That letter, that backward non-apology had been the kiss of death and the reason why I left Vegas and the shame I was bound to bring my parents to move to New York with Millie.

I must have dozed for a while because when I opened my eyes Damion was all curled up against me sleeping soundly, and we were both wrapped in a warm blanket.

I tried to stretch a little without moving him and jerked when I turned my head to find Sebastiano sitting on the seat across the aisle, looking at me silently.

Damion mumbled in his sleep and snuggled closer to me.

"What do you want?" I whispered as coldly as I could. I hated the way he was looking at me, with a tenderness that didn't belong there.

"Indie Row will be okay, you know," he said, his voice had lost some of the coldness it was carrying since he found out the truth about Damion.

I looked at him silently, unsure of what he meant.

"I've hired one of the best urban developers to help maximize the street and an excellent baker to take over for you." He sighed, running his hand on his stubbly cheek. "I am not trying to destroy your legacy."

I felt a huge relief at the news but refused to show him how grateful I was. I gave him a sharp nod. "Good." I moved Damion gently to settle him on his seat and looked at my watch. I'd slept for over two hours, and I was grateful that I would soon be freed from the confinement of the plane.

I stood up and walked to the bathroom just to put some distance between us. I peed, washed my hands, and splashed some water on my face before looking at my reflection in the mirror, unsure that the woman staring back at me was really me.

I looked tired and worried. Exhausted both physically and emotionally, and it had been years since I'd felt like that. Since I had Damion actually, and the source of my misery was still the same.

I let out a humorless laugh. Life seemed to be nothing more than an eternal joke.

I opened the door and took a quick startled step back. "Shit!" I muttered, finding him standing just in front of the door. "Could you not have waited for me to be out to—"

He pushed his way in and closed the door behind him. At least I was pleased that he didn't lock it.

This was actually a bathroom and not the minuscule restrooms you get on commercial planes but with a man like that in here with me, it felt suffocating.

"I didn't know," he said softly, brushing my cheek with his hand.

I moved my face briskly, and he growled, but he didn't try to touch me again. "It doesn't matter," I replied, unsure of what he was talking about and not caring enough to ask.

"This wedding invitation is fake, just like this letter. It wasn't me, Calypso. I've not done any of this. It had to be my father."

I looked up at him suspiciously. Wasn't it convenient to say that now? How to get absolution without repenting? What was better than blaming it on the dead?

The handwriting was too perfect, the nickname was too... and what about the texts?

I shook my head and tried to pass him, but he moved a little to block my way again.

"Calypso, you're not listening. I want you; I've always wanted you, and I would never, ever have stayed away if I had known—"

"About the heir baking in my belly. I know b—"

He grabbed my face and crashed his lips to mine. I was frozen for a second as he ran his tongue on my lower lip to entice me to deepen the kiss, but the hurt at remembering all these memories was still too fresh to let his kiss subdue me for now.

I rested my hands on his chest and pushed him away.

He took a step back. "Don't you feel it? See it? It has nothing to do with Damion. I was told you were doing okay. If I'd known you missed us, missed *me* that much." He shook his head as if he was overwhelmed by my emotions.

I felt myself thaw for a minute until the truth glared right at me. If he'd known I missed him, but he never said he missed me... Because if he did.

His face morphed with understanding. "I didn't leave you because—"

I raised my hand to stop him. "It doesn't matter what happened back then. I can't forgive you for what you did today. You threatened to take my child away without a second thought. You are not better than your father, but I should not have expected anything more. Don't touch me anymore." *I will not survive it.* "Don't try to make it right, it will be a waste of your time." *I can't take the risk of falling back into your gravity.* "Move."

He looked defeated. At least I thought he did because that was not a look I'd ever seen on Sebastiano's face before. He moved a little to the side, forcing me to slide past him to get to the door.

I let out a sigh of relief when I opened the door. I glanced out and I exhaled when I saw that Damion was still fast asleep. That kid could sleep anywhere.

I turned around to look at Sebastiano again. "You wanted him to come, you won that battle but by doing that you destroyed all other possible outcomes. So do your best, get to know him but please do this before we tell him who you are. You know, being a parent is not as glamorous as you may think, and you may change your mind about him."

He pursed his lips. "I will not change my mind. You *both* are my family."

I almost wanted to laugh at the irony of his words but only shook my head.

"What does he know about his father?"

"I kept it as close to the truth as possible. I told him that his father couldn't be with us because he was gone before I knew we ordered a baby and that I didn't know where he was." I shrugged. "I guess he's still young enough to accept it as an excuse."

"Ordered?" he asked, raising an eyebrow with curiosity.

I rolled my eyes. "He asked me how babies were made. I found an explanation. When a mommy and a daddy love each other, they can go on a special website and order a baby. Full of lies really."

The pilot spoke then, announcing we were thirty minutes from our destination.

"Get to know him." I told him again, "But do me a favor."

"Anything," he breathed eagerly.

"Don't turn him into the monster you are," I added and went back to my seat without another look toward him.

Chapter 6

Sebastiano

The box Calypso had given me had destroyed my beliefs entirely, and all my feelings morphed in the space of twenty minutes as I read through the unanswered texts, the cruel letter, and the bogus wedding invitation. All well-crafted lies to make her give up on me, and when I reappeared in her life, making wild threats I never intended to uphold, I played right into my father's hand and showed her the ugliest side of me even if, with her, it had been nothing other than smoke and mirrors.

She wouldn't believe me now if I told her it was all lies, they were too perfect anyway, leading me to believe that my father hadn't done all that alone and that one person who I always thought was our ally was most likely a part of our misery - Serafina.

Serafina who promised me time and time again that Calypso was fine without me and moving on, a Serafina who was the only one to know the depth of my relationship with Calypso or the fact that I called her the nymph of the seven seas.

My belief of her involvement strengthened a couple of days after our return to Vegas when she came to my house and almost burst into tears when she saw Damion playing with Caly in the swimming pool. Then how tense Calypso was when Fina went outside and how, despite her pretending the best for our son, I didn't miss the coldness and even the hint of disgust everytime she looked at my sister.

I knew it well because it was the way she was looking at me too. We'd been back in Vegas for three days now, and things were not at all moving in the right direction. I wanted to pull my hair out having to deal with my territory, Serafina's big wedding, and trying to gain the love or maybe just shed the disgust of my family.

I wanted to confront Fina and the more I thought about it, the angrier I got, but I was going to bide my time; two more days until my mother came back from Sicily, and I could have them both in the same room because if Fina wasn't innocent in all of this, my mother sure as hell was a willing participant.

Part of me hoped my sister was not a real accomplice. I hoped my father had threatened her into betraying us—Just like he threatened me into leaving Caly behind.

I remember that day as if it was yesterday. She'd just given me her innocence in The Mirage hotel room, and I felt like the king of the world as I held her tightly in my arms while she slept soundly. I'd imagined in that bed the life we would have. I was certain at that moment I would marry her and give her so many babies. I knew it would be difficult for me to marry outside the famiglia, but I was ready to bargain for her. I had received a text from my father in the middle of the night urging me to come home, and I reluctantly left her asleep in the bed, certain I'd be back before the sun was up, and she wouldn't know any different.

Except that I walked into pictures of Caly and I getting into the elevator, kissing like two people in love. I admitted my feelings for her and instead of pacifying the man; it infuriated him, and he'd threaten her life if I didn't leave immediately for Sicily in the plane that was already ready to take me there.

Damion was also wary of me, and I could hardly blame him either. I took him away from his life, all his support system without a word of warning. He'd been excited the first two days, but when I started to mention school and he realized the move would be permanent he closed off to me and carried a similar wariness to his mother.

He was just a little boy though, and part of me hoped that if I could gain his affection, I would maybe help Caly see another side of me, and it would give me a chance to tell her the truth once she was receptive to it.

This was why I was now outside at the crack of dawn, playing soccer with my boy after stopping him from waking his mother, who I believed needed a good night's sleep based on the deep purple shadows under her eyes.

I kicked the ball a little too hard, and he tripped trying to kick it back, falling heavily on his knees.

I stopped breathing as he looked up, his eyes filling with tears. I'd never felt anything like that before, this worry mixed with my love.

I rushed toward him and ran my hand on his head soothingly. "Hey buddy, it's okay." I squatted down and helped him up gently.

I cursed internally seeing his two scraped knees, it was nothing really, I knew that and yet I was worried, thinking of all the potential issues these scraps could cause.

He sniffled, and I looked up seeing silent tears fall down his rounded cheeks.

I cupped his cheek and dried his tears with the pad of my thumb. "It's okay, figlio," I said gently. "You're so brave. Let's clean that." I reached around and pulled him up in my arms, carrying him into the kitchen and sitting him on the kitchen counter.

"I'm sorry," he said with a little voice as I turned around to pick up the first aid kit under the sink.

"Why?"

He waited for me to turn toward him and he pointed to my shirt. "I've got blood on you," he added with a sniffle.

I looked down at the few drops of blood on my shirt and waved my hand. "It's nothing, I'm good at cleaning blood." *Too good.*

I opened the box and got the cleaning wipes out and hesitated for a second. I'd cleaned enough wounds on myself to know these wipes stung, and he was just a little boy.

"Mommy blows on it, it helps," he said, understanding my doubts.

I threw him a grateful look, the last thing I wanted to do was cause him any pain. "Okay buddy, let's do it." I leaned down and wiped his knee gently blowing at the same time.

I looked up with uncertainty, and he gave me an encouraging smile with a little nod, and I couldn't help but smile wider as my heart felt a certain pride at helping my son.

I did the same with the second knee and applied some antiseptic cream followed by Band-Aids. "Here you go, all fixed." I closed the box. "I'm very proud of you, you know. You're very brave."

He looked at me silently before reaching up to touch my face.

I froze under his touch, both surprised and also emotionally overwhelmed to have him reach out to me.

"Are you my dad?" he asked, resting his finger on top of the mole under my eye, the one that was a mark of the Visconti and that he also had.

"Why are you asking?"

"Because I look a lot like you and Mommy is sad when she looks at you."

My heart squeezed painfully in my chest, and I tried to swallow past the lump of emotion in my throat.

"I don't like when Mommy is sad," he continued, letting his hand drop from my face to stay on his lap. "She said that she loved my daddy very much. That's why she could order a baby, and she said she was very sad when he left. Her eyes change when I ask about my daddy, that's why I don't ask anymore, and she has the same eyes when she looks at you."

"I love your mommy very much," I admitted, and it felt liberating to do so. I loved Calypso, I always loved Calypso. If I was completely honest, I think I fell in love with her when she walked into my house with my sister when she was sixteen and had just joined my sister's high school.

"Oh!" His mouth formed an O of surprise. "Can you order me a little brother?"

"I—umm" I rubbed at my neck. "It doesn't work that way."

"But..." He looked at his hands for a minute before looking up with a frown. "You are my daddy, aren't you?"

"I—"

"Yes, angel, he is."

I looked up sharply, seeing Caly dressed for the day leaning against the threshold. How long had she been there? What had she heard?

"Oh! You are!" He looked at me with excitement and wiggled his bum to get down.

I helped him down. "Are you okay with that?"

He gave me a sharp nod. "Yes, do you think we can get a dog?"

"I, well." I threw Caly a helpless look.

"Damion!" she chastised him with a stern tone I'd need to learn from her. She gestured for him to leave the kitchen. "Let's get dressed now. You can talk to your father later." She looked down at his knees before looking back up to me.

Hearing her refer to me as his father had an effect I didn't expect, and I wanted to take her in my arms, kiss her senselessly, and make love to her, ordering the little brother Damion wanted before taking her to the nearest wedding chapel to make her Mrs. Visconti.

"Wait, I'll be back, I need to show Daddy something," he said excitedly, running from the kitchen, his scraped knees long forgotten.

"Thank you for telling him," I told her gently.

She crossed her arms on her chest, a defensive position she always took around me now. She nodded. "It's okay, you obviously care for him."

"I love him," I corrected her. "I never meant to hurt him, you know it was an accident."

She let out a little laugh. "He's a six-year-old boy. Trust me, he's going to get hurt... a lot. No matter how you try to prevent it. You can only minimize the potential damages."

"It's a terrifying thought," I admitted honestly, rubbing at my chest in anxiety.

Her face softened, and she let her arms fall to her side. "It is, but you'll get used to it. Trust me."

I gave her a small smile, and when I took a step toward her, she took a step back. *Shit Sebastiano, too early*.

"Calypso..."

"I'll go prepare his things and—" She turned around.

"It was Fina, wasn't it? This is why you cut her from your life. She betrayed you."

She kept her back to me, but I saw her stiffen.

"She did it, didn't she?"

She turned her head to the side and even if I could only see her profile, I could see the pain in her features. "She never approved of us, she never thought we were meant to be. In retrospect she was right, but I wished she would have been more honest back then."

That jab hurt, mostly because she didn't mean it that way.

"Would it have changed anything back then? If you knew who I was, who I was bound to become."

She turned her head again, so I couldn't see her face. I was sure she was going to walk out of the room, leaving me hanging, but she let out a deep sigh.

"Love makes you blind, and I loved you to the point of madness, so no, Sebastiano, I don't think that anything would have kept me away from you then. Not logic, not reason, not pain, or loss."

"*Ti amo*, my nymph. *Ti ho sempre amato.*"

"Don't, this love has no place in my life," she added and walked away this time, and despite the sorrow I felt, despite my need to explain, I let her; she deserved that much.

Chapter 7

Caly

I love you, I've always loved you. How could he say that to me? And how could this affect me as much as it did?

I knew better, at least I should do, but seeing him take care of Damion the way he did, showing genuine interest in him, he was being perfect. It would thaw the coldest mother's heart.

I'd looked at them yesterday playing soccer out the window, and when Damion fell, I almost sprang down, but I saw Sebastiano's instinct take over, he may not have realized it just yet, but he acted like a father then.

It was strange that this secret was out and also a little strange that Damion didn't question it more than that. I guessed he was just happy to have a father, and no matter what I initially thought Sebastiano would end up being a very protective father.

I'd tried to compensate for the absence of a father figure. I thought I was doing well, but when I heard him talk with Sebastiano about him noticing how sad it made me when he mentioned his father and why he wasn't doing it, I wanted to cry.

My boy was now having his first day in Sebastiano's former elite school, and I couldn't wait for him to be home to tell me all about it.

I closed the book I was reading, hiding in the dark corner of Sebastiano's library as the wedding preparations were in full force and had taken over the whole house.

He had told me last night that I had no obligation to participate in any of it, and I would not have to attend as he previously ordered.

I had never planned to create havoc in his family or his life, and had he not guessed Serafina's involvement from all the documents in the box I would not have told him.

It had been years ago, things were different now, Fina was about to get married and Sebastiano had his heir. I was queasy at the idea of my sweet boy becoming some kind of mafia boss, but it had suited Sebastiano and his father just fine. Maybe having the money and power would be the best thing for Damion too.

Fina had been my best friend, the person I trusted the most, and she betrayed me in so many ways. I'd lost my best friend and the man I loved in the same breath, and part of me wondered today whether Sebastiano had been a victim in all of this as well.

I shouldn't go there, I shouldn't go and find reasons to forgive him and get back with him. He hadn't reached out in six years, he could have just sent me a note, anything, and I couldn't forget how he instinctively blackmailed me, threatening to take my son away. That was cruel and heartless and who was to say he wouldn't do it again?

Leopards don't change their spots. Believe what he shows you more than what he says. The voice of reason chimed every time

I let my mind wander to how it could be if I submitted and let him in again.

I froze as I heard loud voices coming into the library.

"Sebastiano, we have a lot to do. My plane just landed, and we don't have time for—"

"You'll take the fucking time, Mother," he said with a cold tone I'd never heard him take before, not even when he was angry at me.

She gasped, probably not accustomed to this tone either.

I put the book down slowly on the side table and instead of taking a couple of steps forward to show myself and leave to give them privacy, I took a step back to hide in the shadows and listen to this conversation despite the nagging guilt that told me not to.

"Seb, hey"

Fuck, Fina was there too.

"Shut up, Fina," he barked.

The room was silent for a few seconds before I heard the familiar clinking sound of ice hitting a glass. I looked at my watch, and it wasn't even lunchtime yet. Whatever conversation Sebastiano was about to have was not going to be pleasant.

"Sebastiano, how dare you speak like that to your family?" his mother barked with anger.

"I am not. You two are not my family, you're merely blood relatives for me now. My family is my boy and the woman who I love because you know I love Calypso, don't you, Mother? You always knew."

My heart tightened in my chest as I grabbed the bookshelf for support. It was funny how he said that.

"That girl was not made for you, Son. You were made to marry into the original famiglie. Your father had an agreem—"

"It was not for you to decide!" he roared so loudly I swore I heard the windows shake. "It was *never* for you to decide. You both stole the most precious thing from me. No Fina, don't try to deny it. I'm not fucking stupid. What about all the calls you and I had when you told me how well Calypso was doing without me? How she was moving on, and how I owed her a normal life, huh? I stayed away because I believed you, because I truly thought I was doing what was best for her despite how much it killed me inside."

I felt tears fill my eyes as I was not only feeling my pain now, but I also felt his. I wasn't the only victim in this, Sebastiano was too.

"I didn't know she was pregnant. If—"

"You think that's an excuse? You think the baby changes things?"

"Of course, it does," his mother scoffed, and I winced. "Your heir changes everything."

I didn't need to see them to know it was the best way to ignite his anger. I moved a little and peeked around the corner.

His mother was sitting on a chair looking at her watch without a care in the world as he stood in the corner, his nostrils flaring.

"An heir you'll never meet," he spat through gritted teeth.

She looked up. "Excuse me? I'm his nonna."

He shook his head. "No, you're nothing to him. You wondered why I sent him to school to start today? Because I want him away from you and your poison. I know you want a grandchild more than anything in the world, and it's something you will never get."

She paled. "Sebastiano,"

"You wrote her that letter, didn't you, Mother? Using your forgery skills. Did you gloat at the idea of breaking her that way?" He leaned closer to her. "Well, I'm gloating at the idea of you never seeing my family because once this wedding is done, I'm shipping you back to Sicily where you can rot. I have no mother anymore, and if you ever dare come back, I'll renounce you in public and shame you in the eyes of the people you so desperately want to impress."

"S—"

He turned toward his sister and pointed a finger at her. "You're marrying into the Garboni family, Sister, and you should thank all the gods above for that because tomorrow, from the moment the priest declares you as lawfully his, you'll have no place in the Visconti family. I'm going to meet your future husband this afternoon, and I'll denounce you. You will never be my problem again."

She let out a sob. "Don't do this," her voice cracked.

"You're lucky I have more compassion than you had when you went to our father to sell me out. I almost wanted to cancel the wedding and make you a public pariah—something so shameful that even that tasteless fiancé of yours wouldn't want you anymore, but I'd rather you are married and gone than you come sniffing around."

"Sebastiano don't," I spoke before I could stop myself.

They all turned toward me, and I took a step forward.

"Amore..." he let out on a breath, his features smoothing as his face morphed from anger to love. How did I miss this before?

I walked to his side, ignoring the two women there and grabbed his hand that was balled into a fist.

"Don't let your anger get the better of you. Don't taint your name by bringing shame to people of your blood. You haven't lost your family. We're here." I added keeping my eyes connected with his as my heart hammered in my chest.

"You are?" he whispered, his voice disbelieving as his eyes searched my face, looking for any sign of a lie.

"I am, we are." I smiled up at him, and he let out a sigh that sounded more like a whimper.

"You are," he repeated with much more confidence now as he rested his forehead against mine.

And I forgot, even for just a minute, that we weren't the only ones in the room.

"I love you," I whispered because it was the truth, of course it was. "I never stopped, not really."

Suddenly I was crushed against his chest, his arms tightly bound around me.

"Oh, amore." He kissed the top of my head. "You're my life." He tightened his hold around me. "Out! Go deal with whatever wedding things you need to deal with and never try to get between my family and me again, or I swear there's nothing this compassionate woman could say that would save you."

"Thank you," Fina said softly, and even if I knew it was directly to me, I didn't move from my position against his chest.

"Amore, look at me," he asked with urgency after I heard the door close.

I looked up, and he cupped my cheek, running the pad of his thumb back and forth on my cheek.

"You're too kind. Those women did despicable things to us, and you're willing to give them another chance."

I smiled and turned my head a little to kiss the palm of his hand. "I didn't do that for them, I did it for you. The guilt attached to it would be too great. After a while, when the anger had faded, you would have felt it, and I never want you to feel that."

"Did you mean it? Are you giving us a chance again?"

"Yes, I—" I couldn't finish as his lips crashed to mine, and this time instead of pushing him, I opened my mouth as soon as his tongue stroked my lips and wrapped my arms around his neck.

He growled as he tasted me, devouring me and branding me as I got drunk on the taste of him.

He moved, and I followed him, never breaking the kiss until I felt like we were falling.

I gasped, breaking away as he sat on the leather chair with me straddling him.

"I feel like it's a dream," he said, trailing his fingers down my neck to my collarbone. "I'm so afraid to wake up and find out it isn't real and that you still hate me."

I leaned down and peppered his face with kisses. "It's not a dream, and I never hated you—even when I disliked you, I didn't hate you, even when I thought you broke my heart, I didn't hate you. How could I ever hate the man who owns my heart?" I sat a little more on his lap and felt the hardness of his cock directly on my heat.

"Sorry, it's just—"

I rested my fingers on his lips. "Don't." I rubbed myself against his bulge. "I feel the same," I added, reaching down for the hem of my short summer dress. I pulled it up and dropped it to the floor, leaving me in nothing more than my cotton panties. My breasts were free and level with his mouth, my nipples hard with anticipation.

He let out a string of words in Italian before leaning forward and sucking my nipple into his warm mouth.

I arched my back, letting out a whimper of want as I rubbed myself against his hard cock rhythmically.

He let go of my nipple and trailed kisses on the top of my breast. "You're magnificent, Calypso. My nymph, my goddess. I will make love to you every chance I get and make you forget a time when you might have been in another man's arms," he added before sucking my other nipple in his mouth.

"God!" I cried as he rolled his tongue around it. "There was never anyone else. I was yours even when you weren't mine." I let out just as he let go of my nipple.

He looked up at me in awe. "Only me?"

I nodded, blushing a little. "Only you."

"I'm never letting you go again, you know that Calypso, right?" He let his hand trail down between my breasts, down my flat stomach until he reached my panties and slid his hand inside, rubbing my soaked slit.

"I know."

He stroked a little harder. "You know you're going to become Mrs. Visconti as soon as possible, right?"

"Umm, hmmm," I replied, sucking at my bottom lip as I felt my orgasm getting close.

"No." He removed his hand making me whine wantonly. "You'll come on my cock, milking it like a good girl," he said, and his dirty words made me even wetter. "Pull up a little."

I tried to move, but my thighs trembled with all the pleasure and overwhelming emotions I was feeling.

He probably understood because he wrapped his arm around my waist and pulled me against his chest allowing him to reach around us to lower his zipper and get his cock out.

I felt the huge mushroom head probe my entrance through my panties.

"Move them to the side," he ordered, his voice thick and gravely with his own needs.

I did as he asked, and when the head pushed into my entrance he moved me back, so I was sitting on his lap again, his length inside me to the hilt—filling me so deliciously.

I started to move up and down, slowly, tentatively. Loving this angle and how I could look in his beautiful eyes clouded with desire.

He gripped my hips, increasing the speed a little. "Can you feel me? I feel all of you. You were made for me, Calypso, no one could ever feel this good."

I let out a soft cry as my answer, far too gone in the feel of him to formulate any coherent thoughts. I could feel all of him like this—every vein, every ridge... I was made for him.

He gripped my hips tighter and as he increased his speed I came, tightening painfully around him to the point of feeling him pulsating in me as he called my name and came with his next hard thrust.

I fell breathlessly against him, and he kissed the side of my head.

"You're moving into my room tonight, amore. I can't imagine spending another night away from you."

I nodded and kissed his jawline.

"And you'll marry me, right?" he asked, trailing his hands up and down my back.

"Yes, I'll marry you just like we discussed, we're only a few years late."

He sighed with contentment and wrapped his arms around me. And we stayed like that, for a few minutes, wrapped in each other as I acknowledged the truth of us.

Love could be sweet, and love could be cruel, but ours.... Ours was just meant to be.

Epilogue

Caly

T*hree weeks later*

"Are you ready, Mama? Oh, you look so pretty!" Damion marveled as he stood in the doorway dressed in his perfect tuxedo, his hair parted to the side to look like a carbon copy of his father.

I turned from the mirror and looked at him. "Yes, you think so?" I asked, smoothing my simple white dress.

"Yes, with the crown of flowers on your head you look like a fairy!" He walked toward me. "The mister dressed funny said to come look for you."

"Yes, I'm ready." I picked up the bunch of flowers that was part of the traditional wedding package—Las Vegas VIP wedding of the Graceland Wedding Chapel and grabbed my son's hand as he would be the one walking me down the aisle.

It was kitsch beyond belief, and at least we didn't pick the Elvis wedding package, but it was part of our plans when we were younger, when we were talking about eloping, and we decided to stay true to our original plan even though he was a billionaire mafia boss.

This wedding was for us and no one else, we were done with the convention. It was just us, our son, two witnesses from the famiglia, and God.

"Are you happy to marry Daddy today, Mama?" he asked as we exited the room.

"Yes, are you?"

He nodded solemnly as we stopped in front of the wooden door leading to the main room. "Does it mean that once you're married you can order a little brother for me?"

I couldn't help but laugh as the music started and the door opened, revealing my hot fiancé waiting for me at the end of the aisle. His face reflected all the emotions and love I was also feeling right now.

"I think it can be arranged," I replied quickly as we started down the aisle, Damion standing tall and proud, puffing his chest as he walked me to his father.

"Thank you, my son," Sebastiano said when Damion gave him my hand. "I'll take good care of your mama."

"I know, if not she'll ground you," he added so solemnly that we all laughed.

Damion stood beside his father as the pastor started the ceremony, and we repeated after him, committing to each other and making our bond official.

And then the pastor finally declared us husband and wife, and I kissed Sebastiano. It felt like everything finally shifted, and the world was back to the right order.

"What is meant to be will be," Sebastiano whispered against my lips.

"Indeed, my love. I have only ever loved you."

"Me too." He gave me his arm, and we started up the aisle back to our home where we'll spend the night making love, saving the honeymoon for another time.

I didn't need it anyway, I had Sebastiano and Damion. I had all the paradise I needed.

"Why were you laughing when the doors opened?"

"Ah, our son asked me if now we could order him a little brother."

"I won't lie to you, amore, I'm quite fond of the idea. What did you tell him?"

"That we'll think about it." I threw him a sideways look. "I couldn't possibly tell him that I had one already baking, before telling you, could I?"

"No, of cour—" He stopped walking briskly, almost making me fall back.

I looked up at him as he stared down unblinking. "When?"

"In New York. I guess our bodies knew what I didn't—what's meant to be, will be."

He swallowed and shook his head a little. "When did you find out?"

"Yesterday, but I thought it would be a great wedding gift."

"It's the best wedding gift!" he shouted, pulling me up in his arms and twirling me in the middle of the chapel's great hall. "Now I feel so lame with just a diamond necklace waiting for you at home."

I kissed his lips fully. "You gave me a whole street, husband of mine. I think we're okay."

He kept me in his arms. "Say it again, wife."

"Husband," I repeated. "You are my husband."

"And you are my life." He reverently kissed me again far more deeply than he should have in front of an innocent child, but it was who we were and who we suspected we would always be.

Sebastiano was not my cruel love anymore, he never was. He was my heaven, my future, my husband, and father of my children. I couldn't wait to grow old beside him and prove to the world that nothing could ever come between what was meant to be.

About R.G. Angel

On top of being an International Bestselling Author, I'm a trained lawyer, world traveller, coffee addict and cheese aficionado.

When I'm not busy doing all my lawyerly mayhem or writing Contemporary Romance with heart, heat and a little darkness, alpha heroes and strong heroines and because I'm living in rainy (yet beautiful) Britain, I mostly enjoy indoor activities such as reading, watching TV, playing with my crazy puppies.

I hope my stories will make you dream and will bring you as much joy as they brought me by writing them.

If you want to know any of the latest news join my reader group R.G.'s Angels on Facebook or subscribe to my newsletter!

Keep calm and read on!
R.G. Angel

Also By

R.G. Angel

The Patricians series

Bittersweet Legacy

Bittersweet Revenge

Bittersweet Truth

The Cosa Nostra series

The Dark King (Prequel Novella)

Broken Prince

Twisted Knight

Cruel King

The Syndicates series

Her Ruthless Warrior

Her Heartless Savior
Standalones
Lovable
The Tragedy of Us

The Bargain

Printed in Poland
by Amazon Fulfillment
Poland Sp. z o.o., Wrocław